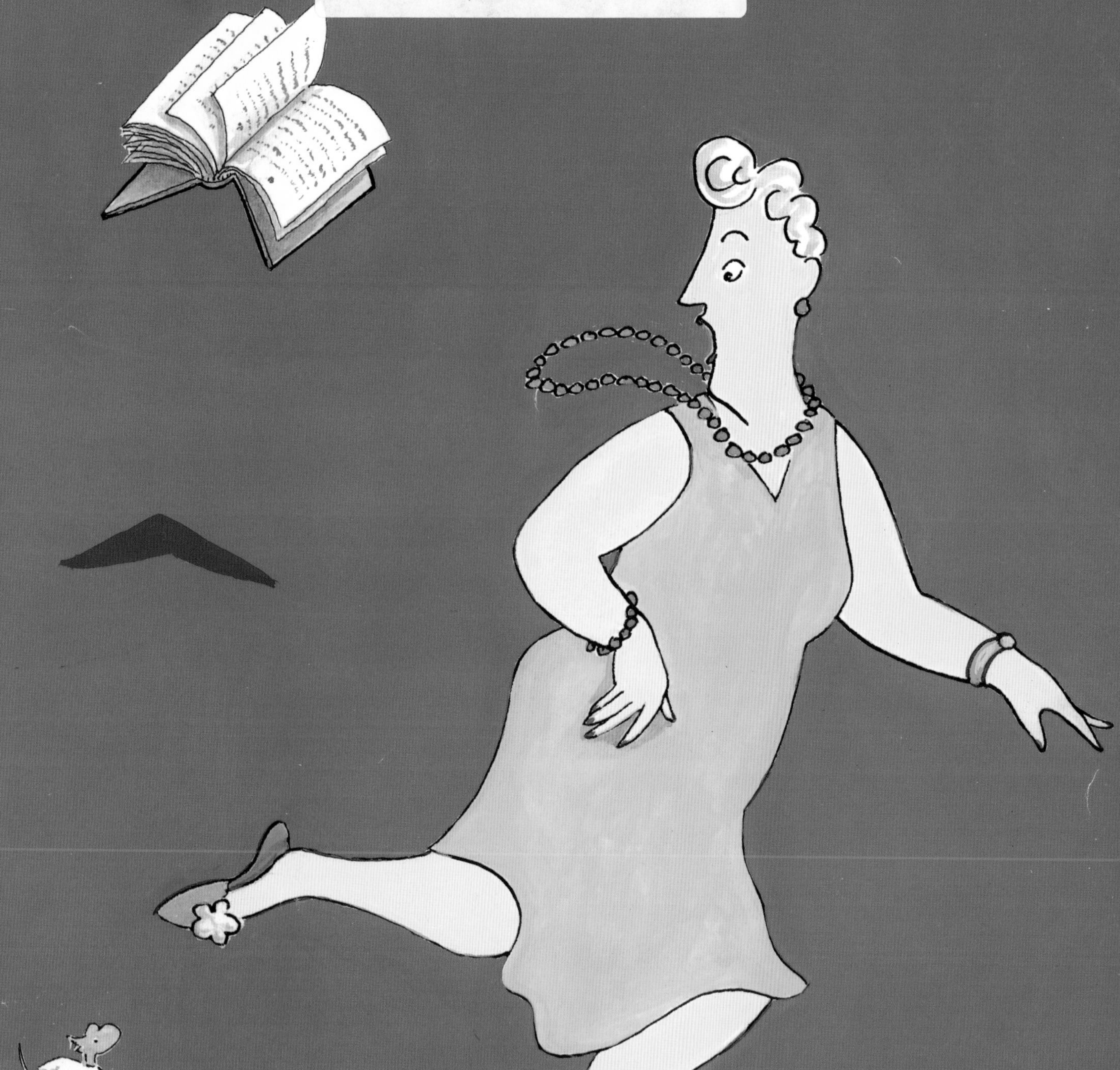

I'm Not Going to Chase the Cat Today!

Written by **Jessica Harper**

Illustrated by **Lindsay Harper duPont**

HarperCollins_Publishers_

I'm Not Going to Chase the Cat Today!
Text copyright © 2000 by Jessica Harper
Illustrations copyright © 2000 by Lindsay Harper duPont

Printed in Hong Kong by South China Printing Company (1988) Ltd.
All rights reserved.

http://www.harperchildrens.com

Library of Congress Cataloging-in-Publication Data
Harper, Jessica.
I'm not going to chase the cat today! / written by Jessica Harper; illustrated by
Lindsay Harper duPont.
p. cm.
Summary: One day the dog decides not to chase the cat,
the cat decides not to chase the mouse, the mouse decides not to chase
the lady, and they all have a party.
ISBN 0-688-17636-4 (trade)—ISBN 0-688-17637-2 (library)
[1. Dogs Fiction. 2. Cats Fiction. 3. Mice Fiction. 4. Stories in rhyme.
I. duPont, Lindsay Harper, ill. II. Title. PZ8.3.H219Im 2000 [E]—dc21
99-39073 CIP

1 2 3 4 5 6 7 8 9 10

❖

First Edition

To Elizabear, Nosie Coattail, Teaser,
and my incredibly fabulous sister, Pidsy
—J.H.

To Ink, Roodine, Dordy, Movadi,
and my incredibly fabulous sister, Pote
—L.H.dP.

The dog woke up
from his nap and
he said,

I don't want to
chase the cat today!

And he stretched a little

**and he shook his head
and he said . . .**

I don't want to
chase the cat
today.

Today I'm going to put on
a different hat!

I'm not going to
chase the cat today!

**Well, the cat said,
Now that you mention it . . .**

I don't want to chase the mouse today.

I'm tired of the running and the scratching.
I don't want to chase the mouse today.

In fact . . . I never really
liked chasing mice.
I frankly never thought
it was all that nice.

Today I'm going
to let him run past
me twice.

I'm not going to chase the mouse today!

Now, the mouse when he heard
what was going on, said,

I don't want to
chase the lady
today.

And he liked it,
he liked the idea.

I hate to see her running
round the place,
jumping on chairs,
getting red in the face.
I think I'll stop bothering
the human race.

I'm not going to chase the lady today!

The lady whooped when she heard the good news!

She powdered and puffed . . .

and put on her new shoes.

She said,
Let's have
a party
today!

Now, please, shake hands for goodness' sake.
(Or let's shake paws or whatever you shake.)

And we'll bring out some juice
and cut up some cake,

because . . . nobody's chasing nobody today!